IT'S JUST BUSINESS

EROTIC OFFICE STORY

HEATHER STOLTS

plicit Press

CHAPTER 1

THE INTERVIEW

THE INTERVIEW WAS today and Katie was trying her best to calm her nerves. She had heard strange things about the man who was interviewing her and she did not know if they were true. All she knew for sure is that all his assistants went on to do great things and she wanted that for herself. She would do anything to get a spot with his company.

The job posting with Morgan Incorporated requested pictures of her. It was even specific to the poses that the pictures had to include. Katie had been told her entire life that she was beautiful, even stunning, but it never really mattered to her. She was smart and that was what would push her through in life.

At 5'9" and a curvy 120 pounds, she had a knock-out figure. It was the kind of body that prompted wet dreams in men and envy in women. She had long, blonde hair that fell in waves down her back and stunning, crystal blue eyes. The fact that she had graduated at the top of her class at Harvard was often overlooked because of her looks. She had moved back to her hometown of Atlanta, Georgia. Aidan Morgan was the top businessman in the city and working with him would guarantee her future. She had to do well in the interview.

Katie dressed carefully for the interview. She picked a business suit but she wore a sexy camisole underneath to help keep his attention. Her roommate and best friend came in while she was dressing.

"Big interview today?" Jessica said, looking Katie up and down.

"Yes, you know that I do. What do you think about my suit?" she said while turning around for approval.

"Looking good. I really like that little sexy shirt underneath. They say Aidan is hot and that he takes a personal interest in all of his new recruits. Are you really ready for someone like him? You are an innocent - we both know it to be true."

"I'm ready to do whatever it takes. I want to be successful and he can give me what I want," she answered.

"If you say so." Jessica did not sound convinced.

The ride to Morgan Incorporated only took about fifteen minutes and she was lost in thought the whole time. She had grown up on the other side of town in a trailer park with a crack whore for a mom. At an early age, she had decided that she wanted more for herself and she worked hard in school to earn a full ride to Harvard. Her mother had died while she was in college; even though Katie came home for the funeral, there was no real sorrow. She had to work to build up any emotion when thinking of her mom.

Thankfully, she had been an only child so there were no siblings to worry about; she never knew her father. All of her relationships had been with older and powerful men who could help her get ahead. She had not gotten attached to them and refused to fall in love. Love was for fools that did not know any better. There were other things to believe in, like money and success.

When she arrived at the building, it was exactly what she expected. It was the tallest structure around, with sleek lines and modern architecture. It was impressive and exactly where she wanted to work. Now all she had to do was land the job.

The secretary at the front desk directed her to the top floor. As she made her way to the top floor, Katie tried to calm her nerves. She knew that he was a bit of a rogue and had a reputation for being a womanizer. That did not deter her; she hoped he was attracted to her because it would make things easier.

When she arrived, another secretary walked her to his office. When he turned to meet her, she was shocked. Her breath caught in her throat.

To say that he was good-looking was a vast understatement. He was the most gorgeous man she had ever laid eyes on. She had to work to find her voice. In the past, she was the seductress and that made her in charge; Katie knew that she was in an entirely different league. She needed to change her game plan.

"Good morning, Miss Williams. It is nice to meet you please come in," he said politely while assessing her from head to toe. Katie felt as if her clothing had been stripped from her everywhere his eyes gazed. She tried to remain calm and in control.

"Good morning to you as well. It is my pleasure. Thank you for granting me this interview. I hope I can work with you in the future," she said, trying to keep it professional.

"I see that you went to Harvard and graduated with honors. You're smart and I know you want to get ahead. What are you willing to do to make sure that you make it in business?" he asked. When he looked at her, she felt the intensity of his gaze.

"There really is not anything that I wouldn't do to make it to the top. I know that every assistant you have goes on to make it big. They can demand top dollar after working with you. I know what you can offer and I am willing to work to impress you," she said.

"I sincerely hope that's true," he said with a small smile. The smile was a bit alarming, but she tried to push down her apprehension.

"What are you looking for in an assistant?" she asked sincerely, which made him smile even wider. She was afraid to ask what the smile meant.

"I suppose the first thing would be loyalty and discretion. Those are probably the most important things that I ask for. We already know that you are smart and driven. I just need to know that I can trust you," he said.

"You can trust me. I am very loyal. I am a very private person so I value that in others. I would always respect your privacy and never violate it in any way," she assured him.

"In that case, I have a contract that states that any verbal terms that we come to will be held as a secret between us and that even if you do not accept the position, you will still honor the integrality of the agreement," he said.

"I will happily sign the agreement. There's not anything that you can say that will leave this room," she said.

He handed over a piece of paper and she briefly read the agreement; it was short and to the point - whatever they discussed was to be private and any discussion of the terms of their agreement would be punishable with a civil suit. She had no plans to tell anyone about their conversation, so she signed it without question. He seemed to relax once it was signed. It was as if what he had to say was so private that he needed to have a signed agreement before he felt one hundred percent comfortable.

"As you know, I am very choosy about whom I take on as an assistant. I have been able to launch many careers and I enjoy their talents while making them into the successful women they were meant to be. With that said, you meet all of my criteria. You are smart, talented, have the drive to succeed and you have... other attributes that I enjoy," he said.

She listened to what he said and then she asked the question that he wanted her to ask.

"What other attributes are you referring to and how would that relate to my position with this company?" she asked, anticipating the answer.

"You are very attractive. That is one attribute that is imperative for my assistant," he said, in a matter-of-fact kind of way.

"Why is that important?" she asked, waiting with bated breath for the answer.

"The job is about being my assistant in every way. That includes satisfying me sexually. I expect my assistant to be able to meet my every need and whim. If that is something that you are not interested in, then you can leave and there will be no hard feelings. If you will commit to one year with me, you can write your own ticket afterward. I will set you up anywhere and with any company you desire. All I want is one year of your services.

"Just to be clear we will also be working very hard with all my companies. The sex is really just a side job. It pays very well and the benefits are not so bad either. If you need time to consider, I understand. Just please let me know when you decide and remember that this conversation is private per the agreement that you signed," he said, very business-like.

Katie had to think about what he had just said. In a way, it sounded a little like prostitution, but in all honesty, the likelihood of having sex with someone that you are working closely with is pretty high; this was just a very cut and dry way to define the terms. She knew that most girls would be offended, but she admired his honesty. One year of working and having sex with this gorgeous man would not be so hard. To be honest, she had done more for less.

"Where do I sign?" she asked and he laughed. He had found the one woman who did not act outraged or embarrassed. She was like him; she understood that this was business with a little bit of pleasure. Now he would give her the final test.

"There is one more test and if you pass then you can sign your contract," he said.

"What is the test?" she asked.

He came around his desk and motioned for her to come over.

"On your knees, now. Take off your jacket," he ordered.

She came over and dropped to her knees, removing her jacket efficiently.

"Take out my cock," he said while winding his fingers in her hair.

Katie unzipped his pants and took out his cock, stroking it a bit to show him she knew how.

"Take it in your mouth and suck it gently. Get it nice and hard for me," he said.

She started sucking gently. She ran her tongue over the head of his cock. He started to get hard under her tongue. She sucked all of him into her mouth and continued to suck gently, teasing the head a little. He enjoyed her on her knees sucking him.

"A little faster. Make me cum," he said.

She moved her head up and down on him, sucking as he wanted. He used her hair to control her movements, showing her what he liked and what made him more aroused. She did as he said and followed all of his instructions. She could feel it building and knew that he was about to cum. He held her so he could cum in her mouth.

"Swallow my load," he said. She did, every drop of it, and then she licked the head of his cock to get all the excess. He moaned at her giving him pleasure. He let go of her hair and she put him back inside of his pants, tucking in his shirt before zipping his pants.

"You can stand now," he said.

Katie stood up and put her jacket back on. She also fixed her hair; it would be improper to go out and make everyone think that you had just given the boss a blowjob.

"Thank you, that was amazing," he said. He was a little surprised that he meant it; normally it took a little more instruction and a lot more time. She was skilled and eager to learn. He was impressed and he was not easily impressed. He had received thousands of applications and she had stood out from the beginning. He had made a good choice. Now if only she would accept.

"Would you accept my offer?" he asked.

"I guess I passed the test," she said with a slight smile.

"Yes with flying colors," he said, returning her smile.

He pulled out the contract and requested that she read it thoroughly. He had some work to do so he left her to read the contract. He agreed to return in an hour and then they would both sign it.

Katie read every word of the contract. She was

surprised that his generosity was not just limited to the time that she would be with him but even after the year that she was his assistant. He would help her throughout her career.

After reading the contract, she was impressed with the terms. When he came back in he asked her if she had questions; she did not so they both signed. He left to make a copy and then returned with a copy for her records. She knew that she did not need a copy, as it was all very clear to her. Her success was guaranteed if she did his bidding for one year. She had followed instructions her entire life. One year of servitude to him was worth making all her dreams come true. It was a small price to pay for her being the master of her own fate.

There was the issue that she was attracted to him. She had never found sex to be dirty; it was just a part of life. With him, she had actually felt incredibly aroused and this confused her. Giving him pleasure would not be a chore. As a matter of fact, she knew that she would enjoy the task. She suspected that he would be as skilled in giving her pleasure as he was in accepting it. The pleasure was something that she did not normally take from others, but she would make an exception with him. He would expect her to give him all of herself; the contract had made that much perfectly clear. For one year, she belonged to him and she would make the most of the experience.

It was not all about sex; it was also about running a business and making it a success. She could learn a lot from him and she intended to suck everything she could out of him.

When the contract was signed, he gave her a schedule for the next week, a laptop, and a phone. He also showed her to an office that adjoined his. He told her that she could decorate it any way that she wanted. It was her office for one year. It was much nicer than she imagined.

He left her alone to look things over and go through the features of her new phone and laptop. He had already entered all of his numbers and email into her accounts so she could contact him at any time. She knew that he had complete access to her and her body whenever he wanted. She did have days off where she did not have to deal with him, but they would be few and far between. She told herself it was only a year and she did not really need time for a social life. This was her life and she wanted everything that he had promised. If she had to get it on her knees, then so be it. She would do whatever it took.

Aidan was surprised at his reaction to her. It was not just that she gave him a great blowjob. He enjoyed her company and the way that she looked. This would be an interesting year. He knew that he had a lot to teach her. She may even teach him a thing or two. The thought made him smile. He had never had an assistant like her. She was so matter-of-fact about everything. He knew that she'd had a rough childhood. Life in the trailer park was not kind to her. She left that life and went to Harvard. She had worked hard and he could tell from her grades and the comments from her professors that she was very ambitious.

The fact that she was willing to do anything was something that he understood. He had come from humble beginnings and he knew how it felt to want success and power so badly. He had made it, and he knew that she would as well. Even without his help, she would be a success, but it would be so much more fun with him guiding her. At the end of the year, she would have everything she had always wanted and he would be ready for a new assistant. He was always ready for a new one by the end of the year. They outgrew him by then.

CHAPTER 2

ON THE JOB TRAINING

KATIE WAS at work bright and early the next morning. She took in the sights as she walked into the building. It was very modern and had modern art scattered everywhere. It was a bit cold, but that mattered little to her. The business was not about being warm and fuzzy. The business was cold and merciless, just like life.

Everyone greeted her as she came in.

"Hello Miss Williams," was the common greeting.

She responded with a smile and a hello. A part of her wondered if they knew the arrangement she had made with Mr. Morgan and if any of them had made the same arrangement. Probably not - they were still here and he made it clear that he passed his assistants on when their deal was done.

When she arrived at her office, she was surprised that Mr. Morgan was already there. She had expected him later and she had wanted to come in early and get her bearings without his gaze on her. He unnerved her, but she would never admit it to him.

"Good morning, Miss Williams. If I didn't know better I

would think that you were coming in early to impress the boss, but believe me you did that yesterday," he said with a smile that made her blush a little. He made her feel like Little Red Riding Hood and he was the Big, Bad Wolf.

"Good morning. I'm happy that you were pleased with me. I hope I can continue to please you in the future," she said coyly and walked into her office without a backward glance. Two could play at that game. He may be dominant, but she did not have to fall at his feet all the time. She heard him chuckle and she didn't know how to feel about his amusement.

She pulled up an itinerary he had sent her for the day. She had most of the day free to organize her office and become acquainted with her surroundings. However, he had scheduled an afternoon appointment and she wondered what it was about. Was it business or pleasure? The better question was which one did she want it to be?

"Where do you want to meet for our 5 o'clock appointment?" she asked.

"Here in my office would be fine," he said, purposely keeping her in the dark.

He knew that she wanted to know more. She wanted to ask him, but pride made her just nod and walk away. He had assigned one of the administrative assistants to show her around and she had to make herself pay attention. Katie normally was very focused and considered herself to be an active listener, but not today. Her mind was on the man in the corner office and his plans for the afternoon.

"Miss Williams?" the girl said to get her attention.

"I am so sorry. I was lost in thought," Katie said, embarrassed at her train of thoughts.

"It's alright. I know it is a lot to take in and it can all be so overwhelming. I gave you the general tour, but if you have questions later then I will be happy to help. Mr. Morgan is very impressed with you or he would not have given you this position. You'll be fine," she said trying to give a little boost.

"Thank you. The tour was great and I am sure that I will be coming to you with a million questions," Katie said before they parted ways. She hoped that she could find her way to the restroom because she had not been paying much attention on the tour and the girl knew it. She hoped that it would not be spread around the office that she was a scatter-brain with her head in the clouds. She had fought too hard and come too far not to be taken seriously. She needed to focus and make sure that her head was clear.

By the time she had got back to her office, she felt better. The space needed some personal touches, so she set about making it reflect her personality. Thankfully, she remembered where the supply cabinet was and where to find the items she needed.

When she finished she felt better and more at home. She could work and succeed in this space. It was here that she would learn all she needed to know about business and success. Aidan would be a good teacher; she just had to stay focused on the goal. When 5 o'clock rolled around, she had to admit to herself that she was looking forward to her time with Aidan. She knew that it had to be sexual in nature and she was a little excited to see what the evening would bring.

Five minutes before the hour, she made her way into his office, ready to perform. To her surprise and embarrassment, he had several clients in his office.

"Miss Williams. Come in and meet some of our best and most trusted clients. This is Mr. Tanner and Mr. Dunlap. We were going to go out and talk business at our favorite restaurant and we would like for you to come along," Aidan said with a smile. He knew what she was expecting and he was enjoying this little game.

Katie was tempted to ask if she would be pleasuring all three of them. It would almost be worth it to wipe the smile off his face. But she refused to take the bait.

"That would be lovely. I am here to learn as much as I can from you and your colleagues," she said sweetly and both men looked happy that she was joining them.

The look on his business associate's faces and the sweet smile that Katie gave them almost made him rethink his plan to keep her off-guard. He had wanted to play a game with her and show her that he was not all about sex. He wanted her to know that he would always keep her guessing, but he could see now that the joke was on him because she had the full attention of his oldest clients. He felt a twinge of jealousy, which was rare for him. He discovered that he didn't like the thought of these two men ogling her all night.

The dark look on Aidan's face surprised her. She had not done anything wrong, had she? Maybe his plan had not been to share her with his clients after all? It was too late now though, the stage had been set, and they had to play their parts.

Aidan had a limo to take them to the restaurant. As they all got in, he watched the way everyone looked at Katie as if she were a piece of meat to be enjoyed. He found himself bristling at their attitude. They would never treat a male this way and it wore on his nerves. And they were just getting started.

Katie was nice to them but very professional. She asked them all the right questions about their accounts, their hobbies, and what Morgan Incorporated could do for them. He had been trying to get them to commit to a new proposal without success; that was what tonight was all about. In his dark mood, he was not sure that it was going to happen.

Fortunately for him, they were so interested in Katie that they did not notice his dark looks or his barely concealed anger when they would put their hands on her. She would discreetly get away from their groping hands without insulting them.

By the end of the evening, they were willing to sign anything that Katie handed them. They signed and then told Aidan that they would have their lawyers hash out all the details.

Katie was thrilled that she had sealed the deal. She could tell by the way that everyone was talking that they had tried to come to an agreement for some time, and the thought that she had given them the push they needed made her happy. It was her first deal as a professional and she felt on top of the world. The fact that Aidan was sending her dark looks would not dampen her excitement.

Aidan wanted to be excited and pleased with his new protégé, but he was getting angrier at his clients' behavior. He paid the bill and then herded them all in the limo. They toasted the deal and Katie was so kind to them that they did not notice how Aidan was hurrying the night to an end. He personally escorted them both to their front door and then returned to the limo with Katie.

"We made the deal!" she squealed when he got into the car.

"You made the deal and I am not sure I like how that went down," he said in a huff.

Katie could feel her spirits plummeting. She had thought it went well. When he saw her face, he felt bad for his dark mood. Actually, she had done exactly what he had wanted her to do and now he was acting like an ass.

"You made the deal and I am sorry for my disposition. I just did not like them putting their hands on you. I don't like to share. For this year you are mine," he said.

She was surprised at his reaction. Why did it matter? She would not have slept with them to get the deal, but what could a little flirting hurt? She whored herself for him. She sighed and laid back in the limo. Understanding him may be more difficult than she thought.

Aidan did not know how to repair the damage that he had done. She had been happy and excited about their success and he had shut her down. It was not typical of him to do this and he was struggling to figure out his thoughts.

"You did a great job, really. You did exactly what I wanted. I just want them to also understand that you are a smart and bright woman and not their toy. It may appear that I think of you that way, but that's not true. I chose you because of your brain as much as for your body. I would never have chosen a woman I did not believe could run a major corporation. It is reasonable to use your charms, but I want them to also see the brains, even though men have a tough time looking past the package. It will be hard for you because of your looks, but I know you can do it and succeed," he said as an apology. He felt hypocritical lecturing her about using her wiles to get what she wanted, but he hoped that he had repaired the damage that he had done.

"I understand," she said, trying to process what he had said. The fact that he took the time to explain it to her meant a lot.

"I will make an effort to make them see me through it all," she said.

"That sounds like a great idea," he said with a smile.

For the rest of the ride to the office building, they were

both quiet. She expected him to jump her bones. He had looked at her all evening as if she was going to be his next meal; he was still watching her as if he was trying to think of a way to eat her up.

When they pulled up to the building, he offered to walk her to her car and she allowed it because it was dark and the parking garage was empty. As they walked, she could feel the heat between them.

This evening had turned out much differently than expected. She had thought that he would want her to perform sexual favors every day; the fact that he did not surprise her a little. On one hand, it made her happy because her ultimate goal was to have the knowledge to run a successful business. On the other hand, she had expected to have his hands on her and she felt a little sad that he had not touched her. She did not know the rules and was even more confused about her role in his life.

When they got to her car, he opened the door for her. He appeared to be considering his next move and she was surprised when he bent down and kissed her gently. His lips felt so wonderful on hers and she melted into him. His hands found her hair and he wove his fingers through it and held her in place. His tongue teased her mouth and she gasped. When he broke the kiss, she wanted more but she refused to admit it.

"Good night," he said

"Good night," she said, trying to keep it together.

"I will see you tomorrow?" he said. He had tried not to make it sound like a question, but it came out that way.

"Yes. You are not going to scare me away so easily. I signed the contract and I will hold true to my part of the bargain," she said with confidence.

"Good," he said simply.

He closed the door for her and watched her as she fastened her seat belt and cranked the car. She gave him one last look before she pulled out to leave.

He watched her car as it left the garage, and then stood there for a moment thinking about the night and all that had happened. She had done what he wanted her to do, and he had been negative to her about it. That bothered him. He was normally in control of every emotion; he wanted to maintain that control. He tried to remember that, to her, he was just a stepping-stone, and to him, she was just someone to help him run his business and satisfy his sexual needs. It was very simple and it had worked well in the past. Why was this different? Why was he standing here wishing he had asked her to stay?

As Katie drove away, she was puzzled by the longing on Aidan's face. If he wanted her to stay, she could not have denied him. She belonged to him for the next year. He had every right to take advantage of that time to enjoy her. And yet he had allowed her to leave.

Maybe he was still upset over the evening? She still didn't understand his moodiness. They both knew that he had asked her to come as a distraction, so why be negative when it worked? She only had to worry about him for another 364 days. She would get through it with a smile.

If only she could read his mind.

CHAPTER 3

BUSINESS AND PLEASURE

AIDAN HAD Katie's itinerary emailed to her first thing the next morning. He had a full day of meetings planned and then he had scheduled a dinner alone for the two of them. He was very specific that they would be alone. She assumed that he had wanted her to know this because of the confusion the night before. He wanted her to know that he had very personal plans for her and she could better prepare for those plans. He had also outlined her part in each of the meetings; most of them involved sitting and watching him work. Observation in this case was the best teacher. She could observe and learn from him and get an idea of how it would be to run a major corporation. Katie was looking over the schedule when he came in.

"Did you get my schedule?" he asked

"Yes. I was just going over everything," she said in her most professional voice.

"The first meeting is pretty cut and dry. I have already sealed the deal; we are just fine-tuning and tweaking some minor details. There will be some heated negotiations about the smaller details, but for the most part, it will be easy.

"The second meeting will take a while because we have not sealed the deal and they are looking at other companies. We will have to make our deal look much better and we will have to suck up a little, for lack of a better way to put things. If we get the account, I will probably put you in charge of it. That way you can do things from the beginning. I left you information on the client and their needs. I want you to study the files before the meeting and if you have anything to interject, I would be happy to have your input," he said.

"I will make sure and study them and have something to say. I also appreciate the confidence you have in me. My first big account sounds great," she said. He could see that she was happy and excited.

"I will let you get to the files. Please let me know if you have any questions. I am available until our first meeting if you want to run anything by me," he said.

"Thank you," she said, expecting him to leave. When he lingered, she looked at him questioningly.

His eyes lingered on her and she fought the urge to go to him. As much as she hated to admit it, she was attracted to him. She knew that would make her job easier in some ways, but it would also complicate things.

"You're welcome," he finally said, and then walked away.

His behavior puzzled her and she wanted to ponder it, but in a few hours she would be required to make a good impression before potential clients and she could not do that without studying the before her. She made herself concentrate on her job.

Aidan was surprised at how tongue-tied he was with her. He had always been the epitome of confidence and poise with women and Katie made him feel things he had never felt before.

He went back to his desk and tried to concentrate on his plans for the day. Today, he would teach Katie about business, and tonight he would teach her what he liked in the bedroom.

Her voice jolted him out of his thoughts.

"There are a few things I would like to go over with you if you have a moment? I don't want to look stupid during the meeting," she said.

"Sure. Come on in and let's get busy," he said.

She went over and pulled the chair closer to the desk so they could both see the files. He tried to ignore the scent of her while she talked. He managed to answer her questions and was impressed with her thoughts and knowledge. She asked all the questions that he would have asked and even had a few that he had not thought of when he reviewed everything. Her mind was part of the reason she was here and he was impressed with the way she processed information. He had assistants in the past who were unable to effectively process information to reach viable solutions, despite all their book-learning.

When they had finished she got up to return to her office. He had the urge to kiss her, but he fought it. He wanted today to be all about business and taking her further in her career. Tonight would be soon enough.

Katie made it to her office before completely embarrassing herself. She was overwhelmed when he was near; she was surprised that she could form words when he was around. She was going to have to get him out of her head if she hoped to make a good impression today.

There was about fifteen minutes before the first meeting, so she went to the bathroom to compose herself. When she came out, she felt more confident and assured of herself.

"Everyone is ready," Aidan said, stepping into her office just as she came back.

"Thank you," she said, following him to the meeting room. Most of the participants were already seated.

"Good morning. This is Miss Williams and she will be assisting me with your account," he said.

They greeted her and introduced themselves. They were all business but still polite. They did not treat her like the girl in the room, but rather like an equal and that made her relax a little. She was more confident that Aidan was the only one who knew about their arrangement.

After the introductions, it was down to business and she had to work to keep up. She had not had time to study the ins and outs of this account because she had been so busy with the other one, so there was a lot to take in. Aidan was brilliant with them and it became very obvious that he was a very shrewd businessman. He liked to haggle over every single detail. The main player in the deal was as stubborn as Aidan, and they were a lot of fun to watch. She tried to imagine herself arguing, haggling, and debating with these men. Her approach would be very different but she thought that she could do it with a little practice.

By the end of the meeting, everyone appeared to be happy. Aidan had sent out for lunch for the two of them. They would eat in the office and he would go over some of the things that had happened and tell her a little more about how they got to this point. Everything was settled and they could start to work.

Lunch was turkey sandwiches and all the fixings, with potato salad and water to wash it all down.

"I hope you like turkey. I ordered it before you came in. If you have lunch preferences please let my secretary know and she will order for you what you like," he said.

"Turkey is fine and I always prefer to drink water," she said, leaving out her love of coffee. He would find that out soon enough.

They ate while rehashing the meeting. She began to see the months of work that had gone into that meeting.

"How do you feel when you do all that work and then you do not get the account?" she asked.

"That can be very frustrating, although it rarely happens. I can normally get the upper hand, but when I don't I can be very grouchy and everyone avoids me for a few days," he said honestly with a small smile.

"I can imagine that anyone would be a little out of sorts. When you put that much into something it would be very frustrating to have it fail," she said.

He was amazed that she understood. Most people thought that he had a ton of money and one account couldn't possibly matter that much. What they didn't understand was that it wasn't really about the money. It was about the deal and the success of the deal. It was great that she understood.

"I'm guessing to most people, all this is just about the money. But it is also about the deal," Katie was saying, almost talking aloud to herself. "Although can you really have too much money?" she said teasingly to him.

"No, you cannot," he said and they both laughed.

They ate and talked about the next meeting. They had a flow going that was surprising for people who just started to work together. She felt comfortable sharing her ideas with him and she knew that he would be completely honest with her.

"I guess I should let you look through everything in private. I have to make a few calls and then we can go in and meet," he said, getting up to leave.

"Thank you again. There are a few angles that I want to look at and then I will be ready," she said.

Katie was a little nervous when the time for the meeting came. She was going to have more of an active role this time and it made her a little nervous. Aidan had confidence in her and she did not want to disappoint him.

"Are you ready?" he asked, coming in with a smile. He knew that she had to be nervous.

"Of course," she said with more confidence than she felt.

As they walked to the meeting, she was lost in thought. She was still trying to nail down a tactic when they walked in. The group was all male and many of them greeted her with appreciative gazes. She would charm them and then go in for the kill. If she had to use her looks and charm to get what she wanted, then so be it, but she would get this account.

"Gentleman, this is Miss Williams and she will be the primary on this account," Aidan said. When she heard the word primary her stomach clenched.

They introduced themselves and when they did she gave them each her most dazzling smile. Aidan wanted to laugh at the way these old goats were falling for Katie. She had them in the palm of her hand and she knew it.

"Katie, you can start if you like," he said, taking advantage of the fact that she had them where she wanted them.

Katie launched into her speech, meeting every question with a quick and clever answer. They were impressed with her and so was Aidan. He had planned to give a speech as well, but she was doing so well that he was afraid that anything he said might just mess things up. He gave her full control, surprised by how well she was doing. When she finished they wanted to sign. He had the paperwork ready but he had never expected them to sign so quickly. She had done much better than he could have dreamed.

Seeing them sign the documents gave Katie a rush. She had just signed her first account. Even though she had gained their attention using her looks and charm, she had reeled them in with her knowledge and expertise.

The look on Aidan's face told her everything that she needed to know. Today had been a huge success, and even though her work on this account was just beginning, the hard part in many ways was done. She had won their trust, now she just had to earn it.

"Thank you, Miss Williams. This has been one of the best presentations I have seen. Your competitor is going to be very upset that you have won us over so quickly," he said with a smile.

"If they give you a problem, just have them call me," she said teasingly and they all laughed, including Aidan. She was a firecracker and they all loved that about her.

When everything was signed and everyone had left, Katie felt both exhilarated and exhausted. Aidan wanted to give her some time to relax and refresh before dinner.

"If you want you can go home and rest awhile and I can pick you up around 6:30 for dinner," he said.

"That would be wonderful," she said, impulsively giving him a brief hug. The electrical current that went through both of them with just a hug shook them; both knew that they were in for a night to be remembered.

She scurried away before one of them changed their mind. He laughed at her getting away from him so quickly. If she could have read his mind then she would have run even faster. He didn't expect to get much work done that afternoon, as his thoughts were stuck on her and all the things he wanted to do to her.

Katie made it home quickly. Traffic was not so bad before five.

She knew that tonight would be special and she wanted to look her best for him. He had given her the floor today and she had pulled it off. The fact that he believed in her abilities at work made her feel great.

She went through her closet and found the perfect dress and matching heels. It was a classic little black dress, cut low in the front and short to show off her legs. The strappy, sexy heels that she chose matched the dress. She knew that she would get his attention with this outfit and she could properly reward him for his belief in her. She also knew that he could give as well as he got and that made her even more excited.

A bubble bath sounded good to her, letting her relax before her date. She wondered if she could really consider it a date given their agreement, but she did think of it that way. As she sank into the bubbles, she thought of all the things that could happen; there were so many possibilities and they all excited her on some level.

Aidan showed up promptly and dressed to kill. He had taken the time to shower and change. He wanted to look his best for her. When she came to the door, she took his breath away. He had only seen her in business attire and seeing her in this dress made him want to ravish her on the spot. It took all his will not to whisk her back into the apartment.

"Hello," she said feeling a little shy. The way he was looking at her made her blush.

"Hello to you, and wow. You clean up pretty good," he said with a smile.

"You're not bad yourself," she said, teasing him back.

He drove her to his house. He'd had his chef prepare them a meal, as he did not want to share her tonight. When they turned into his driveway, her breath caught in her throat.

His driveway was lined with giant oaks that framed the driveway like a canopy. She tried not to gape at the size and grandeur of the property. His house was an antebellum mansion that had been fully restored to all its former glory. It was the complete opposite of the sleek, modern lines of his office, and she was shocked to see a side of him she had never imagined.

Aidan watched her eyes widen at his home. He was proud of it; he'd worked very hard to restore it and showing it off brought him joy. It was his sanctuary and he wanted it to be more about who he was and where he came from, so very few people were allowed to visit.

He had not been born wealthy; his family had worked at a home much like this one and he had always sworn that he would own a home like that one day. The family that they worked for had been kind to him in many ways, even though the lines of class and culture had been clearly defined early on. He was never good enough to come to their parties or date their daughters, but they paid his family a fair wage and were not openly snobby. Still, he had promised himself that one day he would be able to buy and sell them and he had accomplished that goal.

Katie looked at Aidan and he was lost in thought. She loved to look at him when he wasn't paying attention. He looked younger and more relaxed here and she liked him this way. At the office, he was a shark, but here he was something else entirely.

"Penny for your thoughts," she said, jarring him out of his thoughts of the past.

"I was just thinking that this house is probably not what you expected," he said.

"You're right. I expected a high-rise apartment, but not this," she said. "I like this better, by the way."

She smiled and he smiled back. He found that he wanted her approval and that surprised him even more.

"I let the staff go for the night, so it will just be us. But don't panic: I had the chef cook before he left."

Butterflies were making their way around her stomach at the thought of spending an evening alone with him.

He opened the door for her and then gave her a brief tour. He had a pond and gardens, as well as a pool and hot tub. The inside was Old South all the way. It could have easily been a mansion in *Gone with the Wind*. She was impressed and intrigued all at once.

"Do you want to have dinner first and then I can show you around the house?" he asked.

"I think that is a great idea," she said as her stomach quietly rumbled. It had been a big day for her and she knew that she would need energy for the night ahead.

Dinner was roasted chicken and vegetables with a yummy sauce. Katie had never been a cook, but she always appreciated the efforts of others and she picked her plate clean. He served wine, too, and though she normally didn't drink a lot, today was a special day so she didn't hesitate to indulge.

"We also have strawberry shortcake for dessert," he said.

"That sounds really good," she said, even though she was full. She could never turn down a good strawberry shortcake.

He brought it out and served her a slice. He was the perfect host; she wondered how many other women he had brought here. The thought darkened her mood even though she had no rights to him. He saw her mood change and he wondered why.

"Are you okay?" he asked. She realized that she had not managed to keep her expression neutral.

"I'm fine. I just had a bad thought, but it's gone. Nothing is going to ruin this day for me," she said.

"You kicked butt today," he said.

"I did. I had them in the palm of my hand," she said and laughed.

"Listen to you, all confident and cocky," he said and bowed as if she was royalty.

They laughed and talked while they ate their dessert. He enjoyed her company and she enjoyed his as well.

After they ate, he asked her if she wanted a tour and she nodded. He showed her around and the pride that he took in his place made her smile. He explained that he had not grown up with money and this house was his dream. She understood how it felt to dream of bigger and better things. The fact that she had grew up in a trailer park made her feel connected to him.

"I understand. That is why I am here. I swore I would never go back to the trailer park," she said, showing him what made her so determined.

When they got to the master suite, she felt the butterflies return. His bed was huge, a heavy wooden canopy. All the furniture was upholstered in deep, saturated colors. He had a huge marble tub complete with a Jacuzzi in the middle of the room. The bedroom was everything that she expected.

"Well, we have been successful in business today. Now it is time for the pleasure," he said and pulled her to him.

CHAPTER 4

MORE PLEASURE LESS BUSINESS

AIDAN TOOK Katie in his arms, as he had wanted to do all day. He kissed her passionately and she returned his kiss. He allowed his hands to explore her body as he kissed her. He slid his hand across her breasts and down her stomach. He lifted her dress over her hips and ran his fingers up her leg until she found her slit. He slid his fingers inside of her and he heard her gasp. She was wet and hot and he allowed himself a few moments to feel her with his fingers. The more that he fingered her, the wetter she became. He pulled his fingers out of her and brought them to her lips.

"Suck," he said and she sucked her juices off his fingers. He kissed her again, tasting her on her own lips. The taste drove him wild.

"I want to taste you," he said, carrying her to the bed and pulling her panties off. He spread her open and began to lick and kiss her clit and pussy lips. She moaned. She could feel herself building. It did not bother her that she was about to cum in his mouth. In fact, it excited her to think of him drinking her. When he plunged his tongue inside of her, she came and convulsed on his face.

"Good girl," he said. He raised himself above her and removed his pants and underwear.

"I cannot wait. I need to be inside of you," he said and she could feel his hardness enter her. Her body had to stretch to accommodate him. She moved beneath him encouraging him to fuck her.

"Please," she said.

"Please, what?" he said.

"Harder, please," she said.

"Beg me," he said.

"Please. Please," she begged.

"Since you asked so nicely," he said and started banging into her fast and hard.

He knew that he was going to cum soon so he plunged deep inside of her making her have another orgasm.

"Take my cum," he said and he released inside of her. She could hardly breathe. He had made her cum twice in such a short amount of time. She could only imagine what the night was going to bring.

"Go shower, and then come back and suck me clean," he ordered.

Katie went over to the shower and finished removing her clothing. She knew that he was watching, so she did it slowly and deliberately, making him want her even more.

The shower was large and had a rain-type showerhead. It was also glass so that he could watch her. She washed slowly, running her fingers over her body. She spent extra time on her breasts, washing and rubbing them until her nipples were hard. She worked her way down her stomach and when she got to her pussy, she put her leg up on the bench so he could see her wash her pussy. It was his undoing. He joined her in the shower.

"Suck me," he said. She dropped to her knees and

started sucking him while the water beat down on her. He pushed her head up and down on his cock while his hands were wrapped in her hair. When he was rock hard, he pulled her up roughly. She cried out a little when he pulled her hair.

"You are mine. I can do what I want with you. Do you understand?" "Yes," she whimpered.

"Good girl," he said, and then turned her around and bent her over the bench. He entered her without foreplay, forcing his cock inside of her. She pulled away at the sudden movement and he pulled her back by her hair and held her in place.

"Be still," he ordered.

"Okay," she said, trying not to cry out. He pounded into her until he felt her body start to respond. He knew that she was going to cum again on his hard cock. He allowed her the orgasm before pulling out of her and forcing her back on her knees.

"Swallow my cum," he ordered.

She took him into her mouth and sucked. She sucked him all the way into her mouth and he started to cum. She swallowed all of it.

"Lick it," he said, and she licked the length of his cock and sucked the remainder of his cum out.

"Good girl," he said again, and then he finished washing her.

"Wash me," he ordered and she did. Slowly and sensually, she washed every inch of him. They both got out and dried one another off. He carried her to the bed.

"Sleep," he said and she reached for her underwear.

"No. I want you naked all night. If I want to look at you, touch you, fuck you, I will. Do you understand?" he asked.

"Yes," she said. He helped her get underneath the covers.

Katie curled up on her side, sated and a little confused. He had been very aggressive with her, but she had liked it in many ways. She had to admit that some of it frightened her a little, but for some reason she trusted him. She fell asleep quickly despite the fact that she was in a strange place.

Katie woke up suddenly to someone pulling her closer. She felt Aidan's hard cock pressed into her backside. She could feel it pressing closer to her and when she realized what he was going to do, she tried to move away.

"No, I'm tired," she said.

"Yes. You will take it," he said. She felt his cock at the entrance of her asshole. When she tried to move, he held her in place by holding her hair. As he pushed himself inside of her, she screamed in pain.

"Relax," he said in her ear she struggled to relax and take him in. Even though it still hurt, her body was trying to accommodate him. She tried not to pull away because it only made him rougher with her. When he came inside of her, she felt him start to soften. She relaxed a little against him. He held her for a moment, kissing her neck and soothing her a little.

"Go wash," he ordered. She got up to comply. She refused to allow him to see that he had hurt her. She went into the bathroom and cleaned herself.

"Bring a cloth back and wash me," he ordered. She felt tears spring to her eyes. How could he treat her so respectfully at the office and treat her like a slave here? She went back and washed the blood and semen from his cock. He could see that he had hurt her and he felt bad, but she needed to see what he needed and what would be required of her. It would not be easy, but she would be rewarded.

Katie went back to the bathroom and put the cloth in the hamper. She looked in the mirror and promised herself that when she made it through this year, she would never take orders from anyone, man or woman, again. She returned to the bed and got under the covers. She turned away from him and closed her eyes. Sleep came slowly, but she finally fell into an exhausted slumber. She was his for 363 more days and after that, he could go to hell.

Aidan watched her struggling with what had happened. He found himself wanting to comfort her, but that would defeat the purpose. He had to remain strong and allow her to cope with her feelings and emotions on her own. This was not the job for the faint of heart, and even though it would be life-changing for her, he knew that it would take something from her that she would never get back. In the end, she had to decide if the punishment was worth the prize. The fact that she had stayed and got back into the bed told him a lot about her. She was strong and would not give up so easily. She had wanted to deny him, but she knew that she had signed the contract and that it would not be so easy to walk away from everything that she had ever wanted. She was different from the others, and his feelings toward her reflected that.

He decided to give her some time to recover before he did this again. It would not always be like this, but sometimes he needed it this way and she would have to accept that part of him. When he felt that she was asleep, he murmured in her ear.

"I will be easier on you," he whispered. "I don't want you to run away so soon."

He pulled her to him gently. She jumped at first and then relaxed against him. He held her tenderly, hoping that she could feel that he was not a complete monster. He had never cared before if his girls stayed or left, but he needed her to stay and this frightened him a little. He had not wanted her to be different. He lived in a perfectly ordered world and he did not want to feel for this girl.

Aidan hoped he was just being overly emotional and it would all disappear in the morning light.

He fell asleep holding her and he knew in his heart that she was different.

CHAPTER 5

OFFICE ETIQUETTE

KATIE WOKE up alone and was grateful for the space. She needed time to process what had happened last night. The clock on the bedside table said it was around 7 a.m., meaning she had a couple of hours before work. She wanted to go home, shower and change so she started to slip out of bed. An older woman burst through the door with a tray full of breakfast.

"Master Morgan wanted me to bring you breakfast and give you this note," the lady said in a bright voice.

Katie felt a bit self-conscious and did not know how to respond. The woman sensed her discomfort and introduced herself.

"I am Bea. I have been the housekeeper here for several years. I hope you enjoy your breakfast and if you need anything please don't hesitate to ask," she said with a smile that made Katie relax a bit.

"Thank you, it looks delicious," Katie said, finding her manners. "Has Aidan left?"

"Yes. He left over an hour ago and told me to listen for you and when I heard you stirring to bring you breakfast.

He ordered you a feast and gave me the note to add the tray," she said.

"Thank you," Katie mumbled again, at a loss for what she should say to this woman. She had not grown up with housekeepers waiting on her and bringing her breakfast so this was all new and a bit odd for her. Bea dismissed herself and Katie sat down on the bed to eat and read the note. She tried not to be resentful that he had left without a word, even though she preferred it that way. The note softened her mood a little.

Katie,

I thought you may need a minute to collect your thoughts and relax since you did not get much sleep last night. I have to say that I was more than satisfied with your performance yesterday and last night. I hope that you still want to honor the contract, too. Please take the day off. We do not have much to do at the office and I have to organize your schedule for the week anyway. Please enjoy my home for as long as you like and I will see you tomorrow.

Best regards,
Aidan

Katie tried to digest how she felt about the note. It was considerate and very clear as to what he wanted. She also knew that nights like last night would not be the norm – or, at least, she hoped that was not the norm. In reality, she did not have a choice. She had made her bed and now she would lie in it. After all, it was not like she had to put up with him for the rest of her life.

Katie ate her breakfast and was surprised at how hungry she felt. She ate the omelet and fruit and drank her orange juice and coffee. The coffee was wonderful and she thought she would have to ask Bea about the brand. When she finished with her tray, she dressed in her clothing from last night, which looked ridiculous in the morning light. She did not bother with the strappy heels; she just carried them. She took her tray downstairs to Bea.

"You didn't have to bring that down, I could have come back up for it later," the housekeeper said with a smile.

"I made the mess; I should at least clean it up." She did not tell her that she had also made the bed and straightened up the room. Bea would probably change the sheets, but she could not stand to leave the bed unmade and the room a mess.

"That was not necessary, but thank you," Bea said. It looked like she wanted to say more, but she refrained. As curious as Katie was about what she wanted to say, she would never ask.

Bea was thinking that this woman was different from the others. The others had treated her like a servant and had left a mess for her, ordering her around as if they owned her. If Master Morgan asked her opinion, she would tell him that this one was a keeper. She might tell him that anyway.

"I think I am going home now. Is there anything I can do for you before I leave?" Katie asked.

"No, I have it all under control," she said, smiling wider than before.

"I am Katie by the way. I forgot my manners earlier and did not introduce myself," Katie said with a smile.

"It is nice to meet you, Miss Katie, and I hope to see you

again soon. A good lady is hard to come by nowadays, and you are a good lady," Bea said, making Katie smile. If Bea only knew what she was and what she had done, she would not be so quick to think that Katie was a lady.

"Thank you," Katie said and started to leave. Then she remembered that she had ridden here with Aidan.

"He left a car for you out front. He said you could drive it home and he would have someone pick it up later," Bea said, reading her mind. Bea handed her the keys.

"Thank you, again," Katie said before she left.

"You're welcome, dear," Bea said and watched her go barefoot down the walk.

"Yep, that one is a keeper," she mumbled to herself, before going about her chores for the day. When she went into the bedroom later and found the bed was made and the room was clean, she was once again impressed with the lady that walked out of the house barefoot to drive home in a Porsche.

Katie went home and took a quick shower. Her shower was much smaller than the one she had used last night, and it was not encased in glass for all to watch. She felt comfortable being in her apartment. She was happy that her roommate was not home; she needed some time alone.

A part of her wanted to go to the office, but she really did need a day to process last night. He really owed her that. Had she not worked overtime last night? The thought of what she had done made heat flood through her body. She was both excited and terrified by what she had allowed him to do to her. She knew that she could have stopped him at any time. It was not like he forced her. She had agreed with everything, had even signed on the dotted line. Maybe if she understood him a little more, it would all make sense.

After she got out of the shower, she put on her favorite

pajamas, settled on the couch with her laptop, and typed his name into Google. There was a lot of information about his company, but she wanted to dig deeper.

He was from a broken home and was in and out of foster care for most of his life. It did not speak of abuse, but Katie had knowledge of foster care and the fact that he went back and forth from his mother indicated there may have been a pattern of abuse. She tried to imagine Aidan in that type of environment; it actually hurt her to think of what he went through. His need for complete control made a little more sense to her now. The control had been taken from him then and he demanded it now. It made her give him a little break for what happened. This knowledge would help her get through this year. She just had to remind herself it was not personal.

Katie spent the rest of the day in her pajamas reading and taking naps. It had been so long since she had a day to just relax and she hadn't realized how tired she was. When her roommate came home, she knew that she had to make up an excuse.

"Sick?" Jessica asked.

"Yes. I have not felt good all day so Aidan gave me the day off. I guess he doesn't want me to infect the entire office," Katie fibbed.

"He sounds like a great boss. How was dinner last night?" she asked and smiled at the implication. She knew that Katie had spent the night away.

"It was fine," she said, trying to be vague.

"Fine? It must have been more than fine to last all night," she said with a laugh. Katie blushed at the implication. It was funny that she could do those things last night yet blush when someone asked her questions about her experience.

"I don't kiss and tell," Katie said to lighten the mood.

They talked a few more minutes and then Jessica left to get ready for her dinner date. Katie knew that Jessica's dinner would be much different than the one she had last night. Katie checked her email and was not surprised when she found an email from Aidan. He had sent her a copy of her schedule for the week and the weekend. She had Sunday completely off, but considering that she had a dinner with Aidan on Saturday she would probably need Sunday to recuperate. She only had two dinner dates with Aidan over the next week, but there were several lunches scheduled that implied that there may be more than eating lunch involved. She felt both anticipation and a little dread at the dinner meetings. There was also plenty of work stuff, since she had just gotten her first big account, and she knew that she would be very involved in the process of getting it secured and all the details nailed down.

She made notes about her schedule and then read some more in her novel. When she was too tired to read anymore, she sent him a quick email to let him know that she had read the email and would be in promptly the next morning. Her first meeting was with the CEO of the company where she had made her big deal. His name was Mark Station and she would be spending most of her week with him. He had been the youngest person on the team and by far the most attractive. It might be an interesting week with her and Mark locked away negotiating and Aidan being on the outside.

She fell asleep comforted by the fact that she would not have to look at Aidan all week or deal with his control issues.

. . .

Katie dressed in her most professional clothing; it bordered on dowdy. Just because she was Aidan's sex toy did not mean that others had to look at her that way. She wanted Mark to know from the beginning that she had worked hard to get where she was and she was not just a pretty face. In a way, she needed someone to see her as a business associate and not a sex kitten. Her attire was definitely not sexy.

When she arrived at the office, Aidan looked her up and down and smiled.

"Nice suit," he said with a smirk.

"Thank you, sir," she said, refusing to allow him to bait her.

"Mark is already here waiting for you," he said and pointed to her office.

"I will not keep him waiting," she said, walking to her office and closed the door maybe a little too firmly.

When she closed the door Aidan let out the breath that he had been holding. He had thought that there was a chance that she would not show. Bea had let him know that she was different from all the others and he should work hard to keep her. She had dressed a bit conservatively today and that made him happy. The fact that she was going to be locked away with Mark all day had made him nervous until he saw the way she was dressed. She was all business today and Mark was in for some tough negotiations.

"Good morning," Katie said to Mark when she walked in.

"I was a bit early and Aidan said I could wait in your office, I hope that was acceptable," he said, all manners and sweetness.

"That's fine, you are welcome here anytime," she said just as sweetly.

"Now I have the forms detailing what we can and

cannot provide. I am sure that you will have questions and we may have to change a few things, but I am sure that we can work out all the details," she said, handing him what she had drawn up. She watched as he read over them and when he finished she knew that this is when the games began. The give and take and the compromises. She was ready.

By lunchtime, they had ironed most of it out.

"Do you want to go out for lunch and we can finish this when we get back? I get really grouchy when I don't eat," Mark said.

"Then by all means we need to eat," she said with a smile. She was a bit hungry herself and it would be nice to take a break. Even though he was polite, he was also resilient and he knew what he wanted.

They were walking out when Aidan caught them.

"Are you finished already?" he asked.

"No, we were just stopping for lunch," Mark said before Katie could answer.

"I can have lunch sent in," Aidan said more to Katie than to Mark.

"I want to take the lady out to lunch unless you have plans with her?" Mark said, trying to better understand Katie's relationship with Aidan.

"I am free for lunch today, and of course, Aidan does not care," she said, daring him to say differently. They did not have a scheduled lunch today and when she was on her time, it was none of his business who she ate with and at what time.

Aidan felt anger flood him. She was defying him and the only way he could call her on it was to make himself look like an idiot in front of a client. He could have gone with them, but he had already blown his chance.

"You guys have a nice lunch, then," he said, but when

Mark turned away, he gave Katie a look that sent shivers down her spine. She would pay for this defiance and she knew it, but it was worth it to make him squirm a little.

Mark was the perfect gentleman at lunch and Katie felt relaxed with him. He was the kind of man she would be interested in for the future. He had plans and he was going places, and he had impeccable manners. She was sure that he had never been near a trailer park in his life. If her plans worked out, she would need a companion, and a man like Mark would be perfect. She would never love him, but love was not part of her plan. For now, though, she was busy with Aidan, but in the future, Mark might be a possibility. He jarred her from her thoughts.

"Why did you decide to work for Aidan? You could have gone anywhere," he asked.

"It was the best opportunity and I knew that it would take me quickly to the next level," she answered honestly. Of course, she left out the extracurricular activities that she had to perform. That was her secret and she meant to keep it that way.

"I understand that he does work as a springboard in the business, and he is a genius in the field." He seemed to want to say more but did not.

"If you ever get tired of him and want to come over, we would welcome you with open arms," he finally added.

"Thank you, but I have a one-year contract with Aidan. After that, I am not sure where I will go. I can keep you in mind. Maybe I can even take your job," she said with a teasing smile.

"My job? I will have to watch myself with you," he said, smiling.

Mark was so easy to talk to they had a long lunch. When they came back, Aidan was smoldering and Katie knew it. Even though he was all smiles and politeness to Mark, she knew that she was in trouble. She ignored Aidan while she and Mark went into her office to finish their deal.

As they negotiated, her thoughts kept drifting back to Aidan. She silently fumed. You would think that she was having sex with Mark the way Aidan was acting. Why did he care anyway? Ugh. He was going to be the death of her.

When the meeting was over and everything was settled, Mark left. He stopped in to say goodbye to Aidan and they talked briefly. Katie didn't care hearing what they had to say; she left them to their conversation and went into her office to finish up for the day. There was not anything scheduled, so she had the night free. As she tidied up, Aidan burst into her office.

"What do you think you are doing?" he asked in his most demanding tone.

"What are you talking about?" she said.

"He wants you and you just flit around making him think that he has a chance," he said.

"I did not 'flit around.' I made a business deal with him. And, by the way, I got more than you requested. Why are you so mad at me? It was business today. If I was interested in him on a personal level, it really is not any of your business as long as it does not interfere with our little arrangement," she said with more confidence than she felt.

"In our 'little arrangement,' you belong to me for a year. And I do not share," he growled.

"You have my body, what the hell else do you want?" she said, her anger rising.

"I will have all of you until I am done," he said and she flinched at his audacity.

"I think you need to take a moment and listen to yourself," she said, gathering her stuff to leave.

"I think you should do the same. He asked me outside if we were involved and if you were available," he said.

"What did you tell him?" she asked, horrified at what he might have said.

"I did not tell him about our deal. I told him to ask you and you could answer for yourself, but what I wanted to do was punch him in his face," he said, shocking himself with his honesty.

They both stood there glaring at one another. Both were confused about the emotions the other person brought out in them. Aidan had never cared before and he did not know how to handle his jealousy. She did not know how to handle someone else telling her what to do.

"I think I need to go home for the night and we can talk about this more tomorrow," she said, trying to bring reason and sanity back to the conversation.

"I will tell you when you can leave," he said. He knew that he was being unreasonable, but he did not care.

"I think that you better review the contract. I have followed your schedule for the day and now I am going home, as the contract says I can," she said, her anger rising.

"You will do what I say," he said, grabbing her. She wrenched her arm away from him and walked towards the door. He was angry and she was not sure what he would do if he was pushed to his limit. He went after her, but his security guard walked in.

"Is everything alright, sir? I thought I heard yelling," he asked. Katie took this opportunity to make her escape. There was little he could do about it without causing a scene.

"Everything is fine," Aidan said, watching Katie leave. It was for the best, as he did not know what would have happened if she had stayed. His temper was hot, but he did not want to hurt her in anger.

When the security guard left, Aidan was tempted to follow her, but he did not trust himself so he let her go. When Mark had come to him and innocently asked if she was taken, he had been livid. It was an acceptable question and his anger was unjustified. She would be better off with a man like Mark, but he was not ready to let her go. She belonged to him for a year and she was not going to date other men. He would make sure that she knew that tomorrow. After the year was over, she could see anyone that she wanted.

He knew it was odd that he felt this way because in the past he had even encouraged his assistants to seek others to satisfy their emotional needs. All he had wanted was their body and their loyalty. Of course, he also expected them to do their job and do it well, but aside from that, their life was their own to live. The fact that he felt differently about Katie this early made him wonder if he had made a mistake. He liked his life the way it was and bringing someone in that disrupted all of that was maybe not a great decision. However, letting her go was not an option, so he would do what he needed to do to make it work.

Katie left the office infuriated at Aidan. How dare he dictate her life? She wanted to leave and never come back, but that was not in her blood. She needed this and she would not allow one arrogant ass to scare her away.

The drive home was awful for her. When her phone rang, she ignored it. She knew it was him, and she could not talk to him right now. Tomorrow she would deal with him, but for tonight she just wanted to go home and get this day out of her head. He had ruined a very successful day for her with his misplaced jealousy. It was a night for celebration and he had stolen that from her.

When Aidan calmed down, he went over what she had negotiated with Mark. She was good at her job and she had gotten a better deal than he would have. He felt horrible that he had taken that from her. He wanted to fix it but did not know-how. He decided to call Bea.

"How do I make up to a woman when I acted like an idiot?" he asked.

Bea was quiet for a moment and then she replied, "Flowers, sir, and maybe chocolate."

"Flowers and chocolate," he said. "Anything else?"

"An apology helps, too, sir," she said

He smiled.

"Thank you," he said

"Anytime, sir," she said.

He disconnected and called the flower shop. He would pay them a fortune to make a delivery that said, "I'm sorry" and "Please come back." They agreed to take it to her apartment immediately. He called his favorite chocolate shop and had them deliver her some of their best chocolate. He told both to put "I'm sorry" on the cards and sign his name. He started to go over to her apartment, but he did not think that would help. He was the last person that she wanted to see and he needed to work on his composure before he saw her again. He left the office and headed home.

When someone knocked at Katie's door, she was afraid it was Aidan. She considered ignoring it, but she went and looked through the peephole. A man was there with a huge vase full of flowers. When she opened the door, she was surprised that they were for her. She was even more surprised when she read the card. It simply said, "I'm Sorry" and was signed "Aidan."

She could not believe that he was capable of apologizing. The delivery guy had her sign for the flowers and before she closed the door, she received chocolates as well with the same message. After she signed for the chocolates, she closed the door and sat down with the cards and the presents. He continued to amaze her. She never expected that he was capable of such a gesture and that made her think that there was more to him than meets the eye. After much consideration, she decided to send him an email.

Aidan,

I received the flowers and chocolates and, more importantly, the apology. I accept your apology and I will return tomorrow. I think we have some things to iron out, but I believe that we can make this work if we can both control our tempers.

Regards,
Katie

She hit the 'Send' key and then decided to go to bed. The day had left her physically and mentally exhausted. Tomorrow was another day and she knew that she would have to face Aidan and work things out. His apology only meant that he wanted her to come back. He did not like to bend and give and she was not sure that she was the person that he wanted her to be in the office. She would be his whore in the bedroom, but in the office, he would treat her with the respect and courtesy that she had earned. That was not negotiable in her eyes. Mark was going to be working with her closely and he would have to get over his jealousy. As she fell asleep, she thought of Mark and what the future held for them.

She did not know if she wanted to have a future with him or anyone, but she knew that no matter what she wanted, there would never be a future with Aidan. He was not the boyfriend type.

CHAPTER 6

LUNCH, COFFEE, TEA, OR ME

KATIE MADE it to work early the next morning to avoid seeing Aidan. She wanted to be in her office and working when he arrived so she could busy herself with the tasks of the day. The lunch that he had scheduled loomed in the back of her mind and she wondered what he had in store for her. Maybe he would want to skip it after the fight they had, but something told her she would not be that lucky. Her ploy did not work. He was already there when she arrived. When she walked in, he looked up briefly.

"Good morning, Miss Williams," he said simply.

"Good morning," she said, mimicking his nonchalant style. She walked past him and into her office. He allowed her to go without any further comments.

Aidan was happy that she was here and appeared to be putting last night behind her. He knew that he had scheduled a lunch session and he struggled with canceling it or allowing it to go on as planned. He decided the best thing was to let her decide. He walked over to her office and peered in. She was lost in files and work.

"Do you still want to have the lunch meeting?" he

asked, feeling a bit silly asking like a young boy on his first date.

"Yes. We will follow the schedule. I always finish what I start," she said. He knew that she meant it with her whole heart.

"Great. I will see you in my office at about 1 p.m. if that works for you," he said.

"That should be fine. I have a meeting with Mark this morning, but we should be done by then," she said as if they were planning a business meeting. They both knew what would happen during the meeting and it was anything but business.

"I'll order lunch in and we can meet in my office," he said. When she looked at him horrified, he smiled.

"My office is completely soundproof and we will not be disturbed," he said.

She did not know the proper response to that, so she just nodded her head.

"I will let you get back to your work. I will see you at lunch," he said and before she could respond, he was gone.

Katie sighed. He gave her an out and that was better than she had expected. She preferred to keep her commitments and go by the schedule. It did not matter to her that she was going to be his lunch; she just had to hope that he did not take yesterday's aggressions out on her.

Mark arrived on time and he was all business. He occasionally gave her a glance to let her know that he may want more than a business relationship, but she ignored his signals. This year was about taking her career to the next level. Aidan would consume her and she could not afford another relationship. Maybe when this year was over, if Mark was still single, there may be a chance, but for now, they were only going to be business associates.

By lunchtime, they were finished with their business.

"Do you want to grab some lunch?" he asked.

"I'm sorry, I already have plans. Thank you, though," she said. When his face fell, she gave him her most dazzling smile.

"Could I have a rain check?" she asked, and it seemed to appease him.

"Sure, a rain check would be great," he said, getting up to leave. "I will see you tomorrow?" he asked and she confirmed the meeting.

When he left, she tied up a few loose ends and made some notes about things she needed to do before she met with him tomorrow. Even though he liked her, Mark still expected a lot from her. If she wanted to be respected and taken seriously then she had to impress the right people, it was not enough to be just a pretty face. She wanted to be known for her savvy business practices, not her looks.

She knew that her deal with Aidan contradicted what she wanted in life, but felt that sometimes you had to do things to get where you wanted to be.

At least this time she had been given a choice and she had made the choice to be his sex toy when he wanted. He needed control, but in many ways so did she. The fact that she had been approached and given options was much more than people in her past had done. They had taken and they never gave back. Aidan may take, but she was rewarded and if she told him she wanted out, he would let her go. She also knew that he would honor his part of the bargain and she would never have to be anyone's toy again. As a matter of fact, she may have a boy toy of her own. The thought made her smile. Aidan picked that time to come in.

"A smile? I hope that's for me," he teased.

"Don't flatter yourself," she said with a smile to show

him that she was teasing and not trying to start another argument.

"Ouch. You wound me," he said, clutching his heart. She could not help but laugh at his antics.

"Sure, I did," she said.

"I had lunch brought in. Are you hungry?" he asked.

"Yes," she said and walked towards his office. She was surprised to see a feast on silver trays.

"Wow. I was expecting sandwiches in paper bags," she said. She started to make a plate and he stopped her.

"Let me make it for you," he said. He made her a plate and served her. She was a bit surprised that he would serve her, but she allowed it because this was his time and she was here for his pleasure.

He made his plate and sat down with her. They talked about her new account and several meetings that he wanted her to attend. He offered a bottle of wine and she took a glass. It was delicious and even though it was in the middle of the day, she needed it to calm her nerves. She had to wonder if he was numbing her up to reduce the pain he was about to inflict.

When the meal was done, he took her plate, then bent down and removed her shoes. He started massaging her feet. Even though she was surprised, it felt so good to have his hands massaging and caressing her. He slowly made his way up her calves, adding kisses as he climbed. By the time he got to her thighs, she was in heaven. Every time she would try and stop him and give him pleasure, he would stop her and continue his assault.

He made his way up her thighs and she spread her legs for him. He removed her panties and started kissing and licking her pussy lips and clit. She sucked in her breath. His tongue felt so good. He continued to lick and suck and then slid his finger inside of her to add to his assault.

He was taking her breath away. She felt herself building and when she came, he licked and kissed it away. He lifted her onto the desk, pushing papers away as he did. He slowly removed her dress and bra. He took his shirt off and his pants and underwear. She loved to look at him without any clothing. He was all rippled muscles and hard abs. You would have to be blind not to appreciate the way that he looked. She started to touch him and he shook his head.

"This is all about you," he said and she smiled.

He entered her slowly, allowing her to become accustomed to his size. Then he started to move slowly. He reached down and gently sucked her nipples into his mouth. He licked and sucked her nipples as he moved slowly in and out of her. It felt so good the way he was moving and touching her so sensuously. She felt herself begin to build and he increased his tempo.

"Please," she moaned.

She came hard on him and he joined her. He surprised himself when he reached down and kissed her gently on the lips. She was surprised as well but she kissed him back.

Aidan rarely kissed the women he was intimate with, but he had wanted to kiss her and he did. He would think about what it meant later. For now, he wanted to enjoy this time with her.

CHAPTER 7

JEALOUSY REARS ITS
UGLY HEAD

AFTER LUNCH, it was business as usual and Aidan did not mention their lunch session again. Katie was completely shocked at the change in his attitude. He had made love to her, for lack of a better way to put things. He was not demanding or controlling, he had made it all about her. She was so lost in thought that when he asked her a question he had to ask her several times.

"Katie?" he asked.

"Yes? I'm sorry. I was just thinking about all these projections and I got lost in thought," she said, lying through her teeth. She was picturing him naked and they both knew it, she just had to hope that he was too much of a gentleman to comment.

"These projections are very interesting," he said with a smile.

"What was your question?" she asked.

"Never mind, let's call it a night. It's been a long day and we both could use a break," he said.

Katie expected him to ask her out for the evening after the lunch that they had and she was a bit surprised when he did not. She went to her office and gathered her stuff and a few files to look over for the night. She heard voices in Aidan's office and wondered who was still at the office. They were normally the first ones there and the last ones to leave. When Katie went to tell him goodnight, she was shocked to see a very attractive woman with Aidan.

"Goodnight," she said. She really just wanted to leave, but since they had already seen her she had to say something.

"Goodnight," Aidan said, but he did not introduce his friend.

"Aidan, don't be rude honey. Introduce us," the woman said.

"Katie, this is Antoinette. Antoinette this is my business associate, Katie," he said in a tight voice.

"Is that what you're calling them now?" Antoinette asked, looking Katie up and down.

Katie wanted to smack her. She didn't notice that Aidan looked like he did as well.

"Katie went to Harvard and has landed a big account and she has not even been here for a week. So whatever you are thinking, you are wrong," Aidan said, trying to repair the damage that Antoinette had done.

"I was Aidan's assistant once too," she said, winking at Katie.

"I see," Katie said, at a loss for words. No matter what happened, she was not in the same class as this common trollop. Katie turned to leave and Antoinette went over and sat on the desk in front of Aidan. It was clear what the evening would bring for them and Katie wanted to leave.

"See you tomorrow," she said as she left.

Aidan was livid that Antoinette had tried to make a fool out of Katie. She had come to him uninvited, which he normally did not mind. She was one of his previous girls from the past, but she had ruined one opportunity after another for herself. Now she came around when she needed money and he usually gave it to her. He was so mad at her now he wanted to send her on her way without the money that she wanted.

"She's a bit clean-cut for you, don't you think?" she asked, trying to get to him.

"It is really none of your business, Antoinette," he said. He had enough and now he wanted her out. "Could you tell me what you came for so I can go home?"

"I want you, Aidan. That's what I always want," she said, running her fingers down his chest.

"I'm not in the mood for this little game. Just tell me what you want and get it over with," he said, tiring of her.

She pouted and when he ignored her instead of playing along, she got upset. He had always played before; it must be the new girl. Well, that little bitch Katie was not going to keep her from Aidan.

Now she couldn't ask for money and it looked like sex was out, as well. She would think of a way to fix this, but for now, she had to save face. Antoinette had learned early when to cut her losses and go the other way.

"I just stopped by to say hi. I can see that you are busy, so I'll be on my way," she said, hoping he would stop her and ask her to stay.

"It was nice to see you," he said, dismissing her with his flat, uninterested tone.

She was fuming inside, but she had to pretend that everything was fine. If he thought that she would be dismissed and let it go without retaliation, then he did not know her after all. She was not one of his twits to be ignored.

Antoinette felt even more frustrated because she did not get the money that she wanted. Now she would have to go to one of the older men she serviced. She hated their soft bodies, their loose skin. It turned her stomach. Aidan had a great body and was wonderful in bed, so it was fun and profitable. Tonight she would have to work for her money, but in the end, she would make sure that it was Aidan and his little tart that paid.

When Antoinette was gone, Aidan tried to call Katie but she did not answer. He couldn't blame her and he felt foolish for allowing Antoinette to make her look the fool. He could not tell her to stay away from Mark one minute and then have a woman all over him the next. There was a chance, too, that she simply did not care about him being with another woman; that bothered him even more. He wanted her to care as he had when he saw what Mark wanted from her.

He decided to let it go for the night and tackle the issue tomorrow. He had wanted to be with her tonight, but he was pretty sure that she was not going to be in the mood for him now. He left the office alone and went home to an empty house. It had never really bothered him before - he had always enjoyed the solitude - but tonight he felt lonely and confused.

Katie made her way to the apartment without breaking down. She did not know why she was so upset. They were not a couple, after all. He owned her for a period of time, but she did not have any rights to him. That was very clear to her now. The way that hussy had talked to her, she wanted to punch her in the face. The more Katie tried to put things in perspective, the angrier she became. He told her to stay away from Mark, but then practically has some woman sitting in his lap? How dare he treat her like this?

She was humiliated, too, that Antoinette knew what their arrangement was.

Was that the kind of woman he had in the past? Was Katie the same caliber of a person as this common trollop? These questions plagued her. She went back and forth with herself all evening as she considered breaking their contract. She could run away and just take an entry-level job somewhere, but it would take years to get her where Aidan could in one year. If she could just take all the emotions out of it and look at it as business, then she could get through the year and have the career and money that she had always wanted.

When she put things in perspective, she felt better. She just had to keep her heart out of it. When he wanted to be romantic, she would tell him that she preferred to keep it a business arrangement. She would not fall in love with him and give him the power to hurt her. This was a means to an end. He could have all the trollops he wanted; they would just spare her some of his affections and attention.

As she fell asleep, she had almost convinced herself that she did not care what Aidan was doing with that woman. The thought that he could be holding her as he fell asleep was almost out of her mind. It was easy to lie to herself when he was not around, but when the morning came could she still convince herself that she did not care?

CHAPTER 8

ALL BUSINESS

KATIE DRESSED CAREFULLY the next day. She wore a business suit with a lacy camisole underneath; the skirt on the suit was shorter than usual, too. She also added some sexy shoes to her ensemble. She left her long hair down and styled it in a sexy way. When she looked at herself in the mirror, she was happy with what she saw. It was professional but sexy. Aidan would notice her and so would Mark. It would not hurt Aidan to feel a little competition and, despite his protests, when she was not on the clock she could do what she wanted and with whomever she wanted.

Aidan arrived at work before Katie. He wanted to apologize to her before they started the day.

When Katie walked in, he sucked in his breath. She looked hot, and even though she was still in a business suit, all he could think about was getting her naked.

"Good morning," he said, trying to appear unaffected by her appearance.

"Good morning," she said in her cheeriest voice.

She continued walking to her office and did not stop to talk to him. His eyes were on her the entire time; she could feel the heat from his gaze, but she refused to acknowledge his stare.

When she was safe in her office, she let out the breath that she had been holding. Her first goal was accomplished: she had gotten past him without showing how upset she was about last night. He had also noticed her and she could tell that he desired her.

Her first meeting was early, so she went to work organizing her material for the meeting with Mark. He was a nice man and she felt bad flirting with him to bother Aidan, but it was all a means to an end and she had to be ruthless if she wanted to make it in a man's world.

When Mark arrived, the secretary announced him before he was sent into her office. Katie stood up to greet him and she could tell that he liked what she was wearing as much as Aidan did, if not more. He did not even pretend to hide his admiration.

"Well, this is going to be better than I even imagined," he said, looking her up and down.

"Mind your manners," she said, teasing him back.

"If you wanted me to behave then you should have worn something different," he said, only half teasing.

Katie laughed and then dove right into the paperwork of finalizing the contract. She was eager to get past the negotiations and start the real work. Of course, Mark would not be as involved in the actual day-to-day work as he was more of the frontman, but she was all right with that.

Mark looked everything over and then signed all the documents. When he was finished, he handed them back to her. She filed them in her briefcase to go over with Aidan later.

"I guess my part is done. Although I will be taking a

day-to-day interest in this account, so don't think that you are going to get rid of me too easily," he said, smiling.

"I'll be happy to have you involved," she said, smiling back.

Aidan wanted to know how the negotiations were going, so he decided to drop in on the meeting. If he was honest with himself, he had to admit that he also wanted to remind Mark and Katie that he was here and watching them. When he walked in he heard them talking.

"How happy will you be if I continue to take an interest?" Mark said, leaning in closer to her.

"I would enjoy working with you, Mark. I think you are a great guy and I think we can have a great working relationship. As for anything else, this is an important year for me and I really want to concentrate on my career," she said, trying to be honest with him.

"After this year, would things be different?" he asked.

"Yes. Things could be different after this year," she said and he smiled.

Aidan picked this moment to come in. When they both looked a little embarrassed, his blood boiled. How dare she make plans for the time after she was done with him? She was already lining up her next man.

"Hello. I just wanted to check on the negotiations and see where we were in the process?" he said in a tight voice.

"Great. As of matter of fact, everything is signed and ready for your review," Katie said with more confidence than she felt. Aidan looked like he could explode at any moment.

"Well, that is wonderful. It did not take very long at all. I can be proud of my Katie. She was a great choice, I think you can agree, Mark," he said and looked at Mark.

"She is a treasure," Mark said, not noticing or caring that

Aidan was angry and that his tone was dripping in sarcasm. Katie was anxious to get Mark out of her office before it got ugly. She knew that even though Aidan was an excellent businessman, he was a bit temperamental and she did not want a scene.

"Mark, I will get in touch with you tomorrow after Aidan and I review the documents, and then we can start on the actual work," she said, keeping things light. Mark sensed that Katie needed to have some time alone with Aidan and he respected her wishes. The last thing he wanted was a confrontation with Aidan.

"That sounds like a plan," he said, but when Katie reached out to shake his hand he decided to push his luck and hug her. He gave her a brief hug and whispered in her ear.

"I will wait a year. You are going to be worth the wait. If you change your mind and do not want to wait so long then you know where I will be," he said.

Aidan had to use every ounce of self-control that he had to keep from hitting Mark. The guy had some nerve touching Katie in front of him. Even if Aidan did not have an agreement with her, it was not appropriate. He clenched his fists at his side and allowed it for the moment. When Mark left, Katie dreaded the confrontation with Aidan. She had done nothing, but she knew that he would not see it that way.

"That was an interesting way to end a business meeting," Aidan said.

"I guess he's friendly, but he signed the contracts," she said, hating that she sounded like she was defending herself to him.

"What did you have to do for him that he signed them so quickly?" he asked with a sneer.

Katie flinched as if he had struck her. How dare he accuse her of such a thing! All she had done was work hard. Of course, she flirted a little, but the fact that he signed them had nothing to do with her looks or their flirtations. She had worked hard and made the best deal possible.

"I worked hard on that account. It had nothing to do with his attraction to me. We made a good deal. If you do not have any more faith in me than that, then maybe I should leave and take Mark up on his job offer," she said, starting towards the door.

She did not get to the door before he grabbed her. When she tried to wrench away, he tightened his hold on her arm, hurting her. She started to cry out, but he yanked her to him and smothered her protests with a kiss. His kiss was bruising and she wanted him to let her go. He continued to kiss her until she started kissing him back. He loosened his hold on her and he went to the door and closed and locked it. It was her chance to protest and she was at war with herself. He was going to punish her and she was torn as to what she should do. A part of her wanted to run, but the fearless part of her stood her ground.

"You are mine. I thought you understood that. You made a commitment to me for one year and I will not share with you during that time. I do not appreciate you making plans for when you are done with me. I need you to concentrate on pleasing me," he said, walking toward her.

Katie was surprised that he had heard that part of the conversation. Now she could better understand why he was so angry. It was not justified, but at least she could understand.

"So you can have any bimbo you want, but I am restricted to a life with you," she spat.

"I do not want any other bimbos. I want you and I

always get what I want," he said, pulling her to him. He kissed her harshly and ran his hand up her camisole touching her breast. Even though his kiss was harsh, his touch was caressing and she felt her body respond to him. He pushed her back on the desk and removed her skirt and panties. She took off the jacket of her suit and she was on the desk with only her camisole and lacy bra. Aidan took a moment to look at her. He wanted her so badly he did not want to wait. He spread her legs gently so he could look at her. He ran his hand up her leg until he reached her entrance. He allowed his finger to slide inside of her. She was wet and ready for him. He fingered her until she was begging for his cock. He pulled his pants and boxers off and took off his shirt and well. He slid into her slowly, torturing her with his cock.

"Does that feel good, Katie? Do you want more?" he asked.

"Yes," she said breathlessly.

He continued to slide in and out of her still torturing her. He increased his tempo and she met him thrust by thrust. She began to build. She was going to cum. He could feel her building. He started to pull out to leave her unsatisfied. However, he wanted to feel her clench around him. He wanted to feel her cum.

"Cum with me, baby," he said.

He could feel her start to cum and then he emptied himself inside of her.

She belonged to him and he would continue to show her until she believed him.

CHAPTER 9

REVENGE

KATIE QUICKLY DRESSED WITHOUT TALKING. She was confused about what had just happened. If he had been rough and hurt her then she could have understood, but he had wanted her to please her. Aidan knew that he should say something, but for once in his life, he was at a loss for words.

"I guess I will see you tomorrow," Katie mumbled because she could not think of anything else to say.

"I will see you tomorrow," he said. He was just happy that she would be back. He had never acted like this before; he had always been in complete control before her.

Katie walked out of the office without looking back. She needed to sort out things in her head before she faced him. As she made her way out, she did not notice Antoinette lurking outside of the building, looking at Katie with a satis-fied smile.

When Katie got home she tried to get some work done, but it was too hard to concentrate. All she could think about was him. He had consumed her every thought, and now he had made it clear that for this year she could not have another relationship. It was not like she wanted one, but she didn't like that he felt he could forbid it. He could do what he wanted, but she had to be loyal to him.

After a while it was obvious that she was not going to get any work done so she decided to go out for dinner. She felt like a loser for going out alone, but she wanted to get out of her home and be around people. Her roommate had a date, so she would just go stag. There was a restaurant around the corner and she decided to have a drink and some dinner.

When she sat down, she was surprised to see the woman from Aidan's office there as well. She looked around for Aidan and was surprised that he was not there. Facing him was not something she wanted to do right now. When the woman noticed Katie, she smiled at her. Katie tried to ignore her, but it did not work. When she started to walk over, Katie almost got up to leave. However, she had never run from anything in her life and she did not intend to start now.

"Well, imagine seeing you here," Antoinette said.

Katie did not respond at first, hoping that she would get the hint and go away, but there was no such luck.

"Where's Aidan?" Antoinette asked with a smirk.

"I wouldn't know," Katie answered, looking away.

"I think you should. You are his new assistant, right? We all know what he does to his women. You are his for the year, right?" she asked, smiling her fake smile.

"That is none of your business," Katie said.

"I was one of his women. We get together now and then and laugh at all the things that he makes his little whores do," she said and Katie felt heat rush up her neck. She wanted to get out of there and away from this woman. The waitress came over and Katie requested her check even though she had not touched her dinner.

"I know it is hard to believe that he needs to have all this control over women," she continued, even though it was clear that Katie wanted her to shut up.

"Did he tell you that he will let you go after a year? That's never the case. He will give you the power that you think you want, but he will always own you. He still owns me," she said, still smiling.

"It's obvious that it has been a while since you finished college, and what have you done with your life? If he set you up, then where do you work? What companies do you own? Why do you still come around?" Katie said, her anger rising.

Antoinette had not expected her to fight back; she had thought that Katie would just get upset and leave. Now she wanted to go in for the kill.

"Aidan wants me and he always will. He will never completely get rid of me. I don't have to work. I can do as I please because Aidan buys me anything I want. He worships me and I allow him to have his little toys to amuse himself, but he always comes back to me," she sneered.

Katie paid her tab and got up to leave. She turned to Antoinette before she left.

"You can have him; all I want is what he promised me. I don't want him in my bed. But he obviously wants me, so perhaps you need to talk to him about that. He must not be satisfied with you if he needs to go elsewhere. Maybe you should think about that," Katie said and left.

She was shaking by the time she got into the street. How dare that woman talk to her that way? How could Aidan ever want a woman like that in his bed? She did not fit the profile of the women that had been in Aidan's program before. All the other women had moved on and they were successful. Katie had done her research and was surprised that Antoinette's name never came up. It was a puzzle to her and she was so upset and angry she just wanted to go home.

Antoinette watched Katie go with a smirk. She had planted a seed and now she had to let it fester. There were ways to get Aidan back for dismissing her and this girl was the perfect revenge. If she left him, he would be miserable and Antoinette would be there to pick up the pieces. She was not getting any younger and she needed to hook a big fish so that she could live the life that she had always wanted. Aidan was the perfect choice; she would not let him slip from her grasp.

At one time, she had been in Aidan's program, but she had not been able to do the work. The bedroom part was great, but the rest was not for her. When he had let her go, he would still call her for sex. Until this Katie had come along. Her plan would rectify all that and get rid of the competition. It was going to be easier than she thought to get rid of her. Tonight was only the beginning.

Katie slept fitfully that night. She was unsure of what she wanted to do. If she could just forget about Antoinette then she could make it through. The thought about Aidan and her laughing and talking about what he and Katie did make her want to vomit. It was supposed to be between them. He had demanded secrecy, but she guessed that only applied to her. It was a secret that she had to keep, but he could tell anyone he wanted. She dressed conservatively for work. She even put her hair in a tight teacher's bun.

When she got to work she barely spoke to anyone, she

just went to her office. Her desk was full of files that Aidan had left for her. In so many ways she was thankful for all the work, as it would keep her mind off of things going on with Aidan and his trollop. Around lunchtime, Aidan came in and asked her if she wanted lunch.

"No. Thank you," she answered.

"Are you sure? I am ordering in so you don't have to leave. I know you have a slave driver for a boss," he said, trying to keep things light.

Her stomach growled and he laughed.

"I think your stomach is answering for you," he said.

"A turkey sandwich is fine," she said just to get him to leave. She was hungry, but she would never tell him that she had not had anything to eat since yesterday at lunch. Her dinner had been interrupted last night. She wondered if he knew about what Antoinette said to her. The thought that he knew mortified her.

Aidan started to say more, but she was acting odd so he decided to let it go. He went to order the sandwiches and left her to her work. He had never been good at asking people what they were thinking because in the past he had never cared. Now that he cared, he was not sure as to how he should proceed. He would start with bringing her lunch and then they could go from there.

When lunch was delivered, he took her sandwich and drink in to her. He also had some salad and other stuff for her to choose from. If the way to a man's heart was through his stomach, he thought maybe that worked for women as well. He handed her the sandwich and she took a little potato salad. He sat down to eat with her and she looked at him as if he had grown two heads.

"Thank you for the sandwich, but this will be a working lunch for me," she said, trying to dismiss him.

"I want to have lunch with you," he said, and she knew that there was no reason to argue.

"You're the boss," she said, eating while she looked through a file.

He grabbed the file from her hands. When she looked at him, he wanted to kiss her.

"I want your attention," he demanded.

"What do you want? A blow job? Do you want to fuck me on the desk? Just tell me so I can do it and get back to my job," she said to him with a blank look on her face.

He was surprised at her outburst. It was not like her to be this way and even though he had not known her for very long, he knew that she was upset about something other than yesterday.

"A blow job would be nice, but right now I just want to talk to you about the account you signed yesterday. Is that okay or was your heart set on the blow job?" he asked in a calm voice.

Katie was surprised that he was not pissed at her outburst. She wanted to argue with him but decided to let it go.

"What do you want to discuss?" she asked, trying to remain calm and collected.

"You did a great job and the deal was far better than anyone else could have done," he said.

"Thank you," she said, embarrassed at the compliment. She wanted to be mad at him.

"Our legal department is putting everything in motion and if they have any questions I have directed them to you. I hope that will be acceptable to you?" he asked.

"Yes. I want to be involved in any changes or alterations of the contract," she said.

"I have already informed them as such. I did not change

anything, you were pretty thorough." She brightened at his praise and he continued. "You are here because I know that you are an asset to my business and you will go far in this business." It was as close to an apology that he could give.

"It is what I have always wanted," Katie said.

She found that she was starving and she ate every bite of her lunch. He smiled at her and she smiled back. For the first time in days, she felt like this could work and that Aidan really respected her for the work that she could do. Antoinette was far from her mind as she finished talking to him about her ideas for a new project and what she was going to do with the project that she and Mark were working on. The conversation flowed naturally and he was impressed with her ideas and strategies.

After lunch, he left and she went back to work feeling better. The food and the conversation had made a huge difference in how she felt about her job and her future. Around 5 o'clock, everyone was leaving but she wanted to stay and finish a brief that she was reviewing. When she worked she could get lost in it and forget the time. When she had fixed the brief, adjusting some of the finer details, she was finally ready to go home. It had been a very productive day and she knew that she was where she was supposed to be for now. The girl from the trailer park was gone.

She was surprised to hear voices from the next office. When she walked in to see Aidan talking to Antoinette, she wanted to crawl in a hole. Aidan did not see her, but Antoinette did.

She smiled at Katie as she walked out the door. Perhaps her revenge was complete, after all. She wanted Aidan's attention and there was no room in his life for another woman. It was okay for him to have his little trollops, but when he actually liked someone then she could not sit idly by. Aidan was her cash cow and she intended to keep him for herself. He was also a fantastic lover. Most of the men that she messed with were not half as good-looking as Aidan and she would do whatever she had to keep him.

CHAPTER 10

I QUIT!

KATIE LEFT the office in a hurry, but she could not get the image of Antoinette and Aidan out of her mind. She could picture them laughing at her and talking about how stupid she was for falling for Aidan's kind words. When she got home, she had a message from Mark - she had given him her home number in case he had an emergency. When she called him back, he was his usual charming self.

"Hello. I just wanted to know if you would like to go out for dinner?" he asked.

At first, she thought of saying no, but then she remembered her day with Aidan and his betrayal.

"Sure," she answered.

He seemed surprised, but he got her address and told her he would pick up her at 6 p.m.

Katie took a shower and dressed for dinner. She wanted to look good for him. He could help her if she decided to leave her position with Aidan, and even if she stayed, he could be an ally. His account was a big one and his influence could be huge.

She was ready on time and was happy with what she

saw in the mirror. Her hair was left down and flowed down her back in silky waves. Her dress was short and showed off her legs. The color made her eyes stand out. Her mind flitted to Aidan and she quickly pushed him from her mind.

Mark was on time and his eyes told her he was pleased with what he saw.

"You look beautiful," he said simply.

"Thank you," she said, gathering her purse so they could leave.

"I brought the limousine so I could concentrate on you instead of driving. I hope that is acceptable for you?" he said and she smiled.

"It's great," she said feeling unsure as to what to say.

As they rode to the restaurant, they talked about work and what they wanted for the future. He was as ambitious as she was and she could respect that about him. Even though he came from money, he wanted to prove himself to his family, so he had taken a job outside of his family business. The more she heard the more impressed she was with him.

"You could always come and work for me. My company would love to have you. They were very happy with your presentation and they would snap you away from Aidan in an instant," he said, trying to gauge her reaction.

"Thank you. It might be something I would consider if not for my contract with Aidan. I'm not sure how willing he would be to release me and I really don't want to start my career off with a broken contract," she said, but in her heart, a part of her wanted to accept his offer and get away from Aidan.

"People break contracts all the time, it is a tough world and to be honest it would actually look good for you to jump ship," he said, but he dropped the subject.

Katie thought about what he said while she ate dinner. Would it really be all right to leave and go to another company? If so, did she want to leave and start over where she would not be forced to perform sexual favors? The question also flitted through her mind that she was not really forced and when Aidan was being the person she wanted him to be then she was more than willing.

"What is going on in that pretty head of yours?" Mark asked.

"I was just thinking about my contract and if I would rather work for you," she said honestly.

"I have planted a seed and now all I have to do is let it grow," he said with a huge smile.

"If it was a real offer, then I will consider it and let you know," she said.

"It was a real offer and if you want to know more I would be happy to meet with you in a more official capacity. I think we make a great team. We might even be able to take over the world," he said.

She laughed and then she noticed someone out of the corner of her eye. She noticed him because he was walking toward them. By the time she realized that it was a very pissed off Aidan, he was at the table.

"I see that you cannot follow instructions," Aidan said to her.

"I am not allowed to eat dinner?" she asked, looking at him and meeting his angry stare with one of her own.

"You know what I mean," he said.

"Aidan, is there a problem?" Mark asked, confused and a little angry. He did not like the way Aidan was treating Katie and he would not stand by and allow him to bully her. He had heard rumors that Aidan was possessive, but this was ridiculous.

"This does not concern you, Mark, and I really need you to stay out of it. This is between me and Katie," he said with a voice that was laced in steel.

"Katie, unless you want your date to know some things that I am sure you would rather keep private, I strongly suggest you come with me," he said. She started to protest. When she saw the look on his face, she decided that it would be more appropriate to have this conversation somewhere a little more private.

"Mark, I am so sorry. I think I should go. Can I have a rain check?" she asked, smiling at him.

"Are you sure? You don't have to go with him. I'm not afraid of him," Mark said looking at Aidan.

"You should be," Aidan said, and before either of them could react, Katie got up to leave.

"This is my fight, Mark, and I am fine," Katie said and this time she grabbed Aidan's arm and started to pull him away. She was furious with him and she would let him know as soon as they got away from everyone. Maybe she would take Mark's job offer. When they got to the car, Katie exploded.

"What the hell are you doing?" she yelled at him.

"I told you not to go out with him and what do you do? You go out with him! Did you think that I would not find out? There is nothing that I will not find out," he said to her.

"Are you having me followed? Are you stalking me? Because if you are, that is crazy. You know that right?" she asked.

"I am not stalking you, but I have people watching you. For protection."

"Protection? I need protection from you." She turned away from him.

"You have no idea how true that is right now," he said, matching her tone.

"Where are you taking me? Or am I not allowed to ask?" she asked.

"To my home, where we can talk and I can go over the rules of your employment with you," he said.

They were silent for the rest of the drive, both lost in their own thoughts. Katie knew that she should probably be afraid of him and his angry outbursts, but she was not. If she had any sense, she would have stayed with Mark at the restaurant. However, she was accustomed to fighting her own battles; this was a problem of her making, so she would be the one to solve it. She had never really wanted a knight in shining armor. She had learned long ago that in the end, you had to save yourself and it was stupid to rely on anyone else.

Aidan was thinking about her, as well. He had been enraged when he saw her out with Mark, laughing and enjoying dinner. He had never reacted like this before. He had never really cared what any of his assistants did outside of work; in fact, many of them had boyfriends and other people in their lives. It had never been a part of his contract that they had to be exclusive to him. So why did he demand that from Katie?

When they pulled up in front of the house, he walked around and opened the door for her.

"You're a gentleman now?" she questioned sarcastically.

"Make no mistake, I am not now, nor will I ever be, a gentleman." He scooped her up into his arms.

She started to fight him but knew that it was useless, so she allowed him to carry her into the house and up the stairs into the bedroom.

"Do you really think this is the best place to have a serious conversation?" she asked, looking at the bed.

"I think this is the perfect place to show you where you belong and that you belong to me," he said, and then he tossed her on the bed. She backed away from him.

"You are not getting away so easily," he said, jerking her to him and kissing her hard on the mouth. She tried to squirm away, but he tightened his hold until he got the response he wanted. He reached down and grabbed her dress. With one swift rip, he tore it from her body.

"I have to see you," he said breathlessly. He undid her bra and removed her panties. She wanted to have the strength to fight him and tell him to stop, but once he touched her, she was lost to him and she could not resist. His fingers found her and he plunged them deep inside her wet pussy. She responded to him, fucking his fingers until she came.

"I want you, Katie. If you want me to stop, tell me now while I have an ounce of self-control," he said.

"Don't stop," she said and he kissed her again. She felt his hard cock on her leg and she wanted it inside of her. She moved forward and he slid inside of her. She clenched around him and it was his undoing. He pounded into her hard and fast. He reached down and pinched her nipple and she cried out in pain and pleasure. He continued to pinch and fondle her breast and nipples until they both came. He collapsed on top of her and then rolled over and pulled her onto his chest.

"You are mine," he said and she did not argue with him. How could she argue when all he had to do was touch her and she responded to him?

She laid on his chest and thought of what had just happened. He had not forced her, he had given her the option to stop and she had told him to continue. Her breasts were sore from his fingers, but the pleasure he gave superseded the pain. How had he managed to turn her into his whore in such a short amount of time?

He did own her and that scared her more than anything. Would staying with him rob her of herself? Was her career and money really worth all that?

She allowed him to hold her until he fell asleep. When she knew he was fast asleep, she got out of the bed and took her clothing to the bathroom. She dressed and then snuck downstairs. Her cell phone was in her purse, so she called a cab and waited for them out front. He would be livid when he woke up alone, but she could not stay and allow him to take more of her. The thought of him laughing at her with Antoinette brought tears to her eyes. She could not allow him to make a fool out of her anymore. It was time she took control of herself. He would not own her any longer.

When the cab came, she looked back at the house with longing. A part of her wanted to go back in and fall asleep on his chest. But she knew that she could not stay. If it had not been for Antoinette and the things she had told her, Katie would consider it. But she would not allow him to use her for the amusement of him and his little trollop. Her struggles had been long and hard and she had not come this far for that.

As she pulled away she silent said goodbye to him. There would be another confrontation, but it would not be in his bedroom. It would be in the boardroom, where she would take back control of her life and then move on. There had to be a better way to make it in the business world. Falling in love was not part of business and she knew that now.

CHAPTER 11

LIES

AIDAN WAS SURPRISED to wake up alone. He was also a little disappointed. The feelings he had for her surprised him and disturbed him, but he was tired of fighting his emotions. He wanted her and it was time for them to both accept what they had. After finding his cell phone, he tried to call her but she did not answer. When he checked his email, he had an email from her.

Dear Aidan,

I am writing this letter to inform you that I would like to cancel our contract. Many things have been brought to my attention that bothers me and they are things that I cannot live with. I hope you will accept my resignation and allow me to end our contract without a fight. I am truly sorry.

Sincerely,
Katie

Aidan felt like he was having a heart attack. How could she just leave him now? What happened that was so bad that she would want to quit her job and walk away from him?

He had pushed her too far and he had to fix it quickly before it was too late. He wondered if Mark had offered her a job. If he had, he was going to pay for the betrayal. He decided to visit her and make her tell him what was going on. She was going to answer him, face to face, and tell him what he had done that was so bad.

Katie sent the email to Aidan, feeling sad and conflicted about it. If she was honest with herself, she would admit that she had feelings for him and that was why she felt so strongly that she had to leave and move on. It would break her heart day after day to see him with Antoinette and to think of the things he told her about their relationship. She could live with the sex and even the fact that he was controlling, but making fun of her to his girlfriend was too much to bear.

She also sent an email to Mark letting him know that she was leaving and that if he was interested, she needed a job. After she was finished, she felt mentally drained and she went to the bathroom to take a bubble bath. A bubble bath and a good book was just what she needed to mend her broken heart.

She settled into her bath with her book when she heard someone beating at her door. There was no question in her mind as to who it was and she tried really hard to ignore him.

"You can open the door or I can break it down. I really don't care which you choose," he said, his voice booming.

"I'm coming," she said and quickly dressed.

When she opened the door, he was standing there as angry as she had ever seen him.

"An email? You tell me that you are done with me in an email?" he yelled.

"It was easier that way," she said, trying to stay calm.

"Easier for you, maybe. I deserve an explanation!" he said.

"Why? So you can run to your girlfriend and you can laugh at stupid, little Katie doing your bidding? You promised me that our arrangement would be private and then you discussed it with that trollop. So don't yell at me about broken promises. You did it first," she said in a tight voice.

"My girlfriend? What the hell are you talking about?" he said, puzzled by her accusations.

"Antoinette," she said as if it should have been obvious.

"I think you have bad information. Antoinette is not my girlfriend and she never was. She knows about the program because she worked for me briefly, until I figured out how deceitful she is. I paid her for the year and she walked away. Yes, we've had sex since then, but she always wants money and favors and I'm tired of her and her greedy ways. If she told you she was anything to me, she lied." Things started falling into place.

"She told me that you laughed at me and how I felt. That you told her everything about us and I was just a game you were playing," she said with tears in her eyes.

Aidan's face clouded with anger. That little whore had dared to say that to Katie and try to ruin things with the only person he had ever cared about?

"I will fix things with her. And I can assure you that when I am done with her, she will never spew her venom to you again. Please say that we can at least talk this through," he said.

"She lied?" she asked.

"Yes, and if you need to hear that from her I can make her tell you," he said.

Katie looked into his eyes and she knew that he was telling the truth. Antoinette had lied.

"We can talk. I don't want to leave," she said.

"I need to go and talk to Antoinette. She cannot be allowed to lie about me to you or to anyone else. I have suspected in the past that she was trying to sabotage me, but I never knew that she would just outright lie.

"Would you go to dinner with me tonight?" he asked.

"Yes," she said.

Aidan gave her a quick kiss and left. He wanted this resolved and he did not want to leave Antoinette any room to do any more damage. Katie watched him go and her heart did not feel so heavy anymore.

He had not betrayed her. She wanted to be with him. The job was important to her but she knew that he was just as important. It was not the time to confess that to him, but maybe eventually they could have more than a business arrangement. She could not believe that she actually wanted a relationship with him, but she did.

It was crazy how your life could change in an instant. She had not been looking for love and now she knew that love might be what she was feeling.

CHAPTER 12

RESOLUTION

AIDAN FOUND Antoinette asleep at her apartment. He was pretty sure that she lounged around in bed all day. He was pissed off, to begin with, and her laziness only added fuel to the fire. When she finally came to the door, she was barely dressed and happy to see him.

"Hello, handsome," she said, bending slightly so he could see her cleavage.

"I really don't think you are going to be happy to see me. How dare you tell Katie lies about us? You are nothing to me and you know it."

She pouted at him and he ignored her. He was mad and she knew it so she treaded lightly. His generosity had kept her comfortable and she did not want to jeopardize that for anything.

"I was just telling her how we talked. I might have exaggerated a little, but there was no harm done," she said, trying to brush it off as a joke.

"I know what your game is and I want you to stay away from me and Katie. If I hear about you talking to her or coming near me, then I will have you removed. I have influence with your other 'benefactors,' so don't make me tell them your true colors. You might have to go out and get a job."

Now she knew that he was serious. A part of her wanted to argue, but she knew when she had lost and she was not going to lose her lifestyle over one man. Even though he was handsome and good in bed, she would not give up her money and life for him.

"I will stay away," she said, resigned to losing him forever and a little angry that he had forced her hand.

"You better. If you don't, I will ruin you and you know that I can do it. Easily." He turned to leave.

As she watched him go and she wanted to ask him to return, but she knew that he would not. He had what he wanted and it was not her. At least she still had money and her looks and that was enough for her.

Aidan left Antoinette's apartment and went straight to Katie. He had something that he needed to tell her and it could not wait another minute.

Katie heard a knock at the door and looked at her watch. It was not time to meet Aidan yet and she could not think of anyone else who would be visiting at this time of the day. She looked through the peephole and was surprised to see Aidan standing there. She opened the door with questions in her eyes.

"Hello. You are a bit early," she said and gave him a little smile that made him feel more comfortable.

"I just resolved things with Antoinette. She won't be bothering us anymore. I am so sorry that she put you through that," he said as he took her hand. It was a gentle gesture and not his normal style. He seemed to be a bit nervous, which made Katie nervous as well.

"I'm just happy that she is out of our lives and she will

not be spreading any more lies. Now we can get down to business as usual," she said.

"I do not think it can ever be business as usual between us. Not anymore," he said and her heart fell. Of course, he did not want her to work for him anymore. How could she have been so stupid?

"Why? I really enjoy my job and I promise that we can work on better communication. Are you not satisfied with my work?" she asked, confused.

"I am more than happy with your work performance," he said.

"Then is it the other part of the contract? Have I argued too much? Tell me what I can do to fix things and I will. I'll do whatever it takes to make things right. I really want to stay and work with your company." She was hoping they could come to a satisfactory agreement and that he would not dismiss her. He had seemed like he wanted her to work with him earlier.

"I think we need to modify the contract a bit," he said, and then he smiled.

"What do you want to change?" she asked.

"I was thinking that we might even need a new contract." She looked even more confused.

"What kind of contract do we need?" she asked.

"I was thinking that if two people were in love then they would need a contract to show their love for one another," he said and she looked at him, flabbergasted.

"You love me?" she finally asked.

"Yes. I love you and that is why I have been so crazy. I did not want to share you, because I love you," he said.

Katie could not believe that he had said the words that she longed to hear. For so many years, she did not believe in love and romance. She just wanted a career and money.

Now she knew that all that paled in comparison to the way she felt for Aidan and she would give it all up to be with him.

Aidan waited patiently for her to say something. This could be the best moment of his life or the absolute worst. He had never been in love until she came in and took him by surprise. His life would be complete if she said that she loved him, too. He could not even fathom what he would do if she did not feel the same way. He would make her love him. He would have to.

"I love you, too," she said after a long pause. Aidan was so overjoyed, he took her into his arms and kissed her gently.

"Then we can modify the contract to maybe a marriage contract?" he asked and she laughed.

"I think we can try love first and then move on to marriage," she said.

"I see. You want me to ask you with the big ring and violins playing in the background. You want it all. Well, my dear, you will have it all and more," he said.

It was, after all, just business. But the business was love.

EPILOGUE

MARK READ and then reread the email from Katie. She would be staying with Aidan and they were in a relationship now. He was livid at the fact that she had played him. He had wanted her and offered her the world and this was how she repaid him. Did she really think that Aidan would be faithful? There was not a faithful bone in his body.

At least he would still see her at their meetings. He was going to take an interest in every aspect of this project and he would show Katie that she belonged with him. She would be his soon enough. Aidan would screw up and then he would be there to pick up the pieces. If he did not screw up soon enough, then Mark would have to plant some seeds and make sure that Katie knew what kind of man Aidan really was.

He had pictures of her plastered all over his wall. He had convinced himself that he was not stalking her, that he was only watching out for her and making sure that she was safe. The pictures were just a reminder and she would want him to have them. She would probably be so flattered that he had followed her and taken all these pictures. He even had ones of her in her apartment when she thought that no one could see. He had to buy a high-powered lens to get the shot of her almost nude, but the result had been worth every penny. He used it often in his fantasies and when he ejaculated, he always saw her stripping for him and imagined his cock entering her hungry pussy.

She would be his soon, and he would have more than pictures and fantasies. His cock grew hard looking at the pictures and thinking of her spreading herself for him. He reached down, pulled it out of his pants, and started to stroke it the way he wanted Katie to touch him. He stroked until he came. He could almost see her licking up his cum and drinking it into her mouth. It would not be long and he would have her. He just had to be patient and get Aidan out of the picture. He would do whatever it took to have her. Nothing, no one, would stand in his way. Aidan needed to remember that accidents happened all the time.

Aidan and Katie were happy, but if Mark had anything to do with it, their happiness would be short-lived. He would make sure of it. In his heart, he knew that destroying them would be the only way that he could ever be happy. Katie was the only woman for him and he planned to make her his forever.

ABOUT THE AUTHOR

Heather Stolts is an emerging erotica author of many erotica kinks and sub-genres. Be sure to check out other books and leave a review if this story got you hot!

Visit my blog at Heather Stolts Blog

Join my newsletter for exclusive previews Heather Stolts Newsletter

Sign up for Free Stories from Xplicit Press Authors

Xplicit Press Author Updates

Like Xplicit Press on Facebook

Follow Xplicit Press on Twitter

Readers: I want to expand a few of the stories to see where the characters can be explored further. If there are any of the stories that you would like to read more about again, I'd love to hear from you!

Keep In Touch
Heather Stolts
info@heatherstolts.com